The Snowbelly Family of Chillyville Inn

Hallmark

D1466010

The Snowbelly Family
of Chillyville Inn

© 2005 Hallmark Licensing, Inc.
Published by Hallmark Cards, Inc.
Kansas City, Missouri 64141

Visit us on the Web at www.Hallmark.com.

All rights reserved. No portion of this publication may be
reproduced, stored in a retrieval system, or transmitted in any
form by any means—electronic, mechanical, photographic,
recorded, or any other—except for brief quotations in printed
reviews, without the prior written permission of the publisher.

Printed and bound in China.

CHILLYVILLE INN

To: _____

From: _____

It's holiday time at the Chillyville Inn,

     and the Snowbelly family is in quite a spin.

There's so much to do—who can rest?

Grandpa is greeting the folks at the door,

     in addition to handling his favorite chore—

     carving a gift for each guest.

Inside the inn, there are songs in the air,

as Papa plays piano with fabulous flair...

with a solo from Twiggles the dog.

Mama is bustling around with a tray

of slippery ice slushies

and ice-cream soufflé

plus a pitcher of icy cold nog.

And the tree! What a tree! How the icicles glitter!

And look,
you can see there's a mighty fine knitter
who lives here…
and Grandma's her name!

As Snowbert and Snowbelle are topping the tree,

Grandma keeps knitting—and quite rapidly—

until she is heard to exclaim...

"Land sakes, I forgot–I've got yarn outside soaking.

Kids, won't you please take some sticks and start poking

to check on my red and green dye?"

So Snowbelle and Snowbert go out by the barn

and start stirring and swirling the two vats of yarn–

and holding up strands to the sky.

When who should appear as if out of the blue?

Jingles the mischievous kitten–that's who.

(Last seen, she was napping in bed.)

Miss Jingles jumps up with spectacular speed,

gets tangled in yarn like a cat tumbleweed,

and when she rolls out, she's bright red!

Well, Twiggles the dog simply can't be outdone.

He figures that **he** is the Master of Fun

and wants to be part of the scene.

So he lurches and lunges at Jingles the cat,

tips over a vat with a very big splat–

and now he is totally green!

When Snowbert and Snowbelle catch up with their pets,

they hold them and scold them, expressing regrets,

all gathered around in a huddle.

Then they look at each other and whisper, "No way!

What will we do? What will Ma and Pa say?

We look like a red and green muddle!"

They troop back inside, and all four fear the worst...

...but when Ma and Pa see them, they can't help but burst

into laughter and blurt out with glee,

"You look just like Christmas! Well, what do you know!

These things tend to happen when you're made of snow.

We need pictures! Most definitely!"

Then Grandpa booms out, to the whole room's delight,

"Hey, don't forget that it's Gift-Giving Night!

Is everyone ready to start?"

A mad scramble ensues, and more fun is unloosed...

...as presents, once hidden, are quickly produced.

Oh, here comes the really good part...

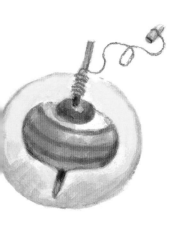

Everyone's thrilled with the gifts they receive,

especially the Snowbelly kids, who believe

that **this** is their best Christmas ever.

On his icicle bicycle, Snowbert goes riding—

he's popping those wheelies! He's hopping! He's sliding!

Does he plan on stopping? No, never!

And Snowbelle can do what she's wished for so long–
with her fresh frozen flute, she performs a sweet song
and melts every heart in the place.

There's a hush in the room, then a voice from the hall
says, "Let's raise a glass to the best inn of all!"
And a smile spreads across every face.

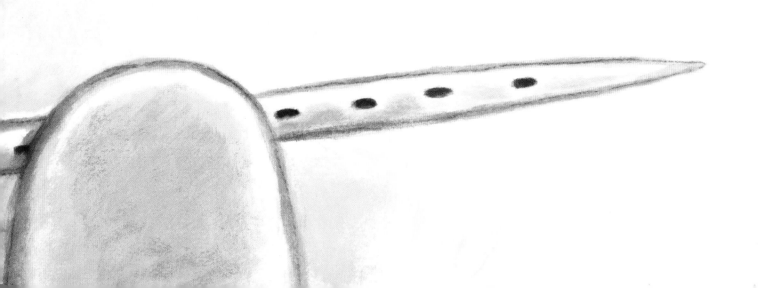

"To the Snowbelly family, for all their good cheer,

and to Chillyville Inn, where we're welcome each year!

A toast to our wonderful hosts!"

Then as night starts to fall like a big snowy feather,

they all share a hug 'cause they're happy together...

And **that** is what matters the most.

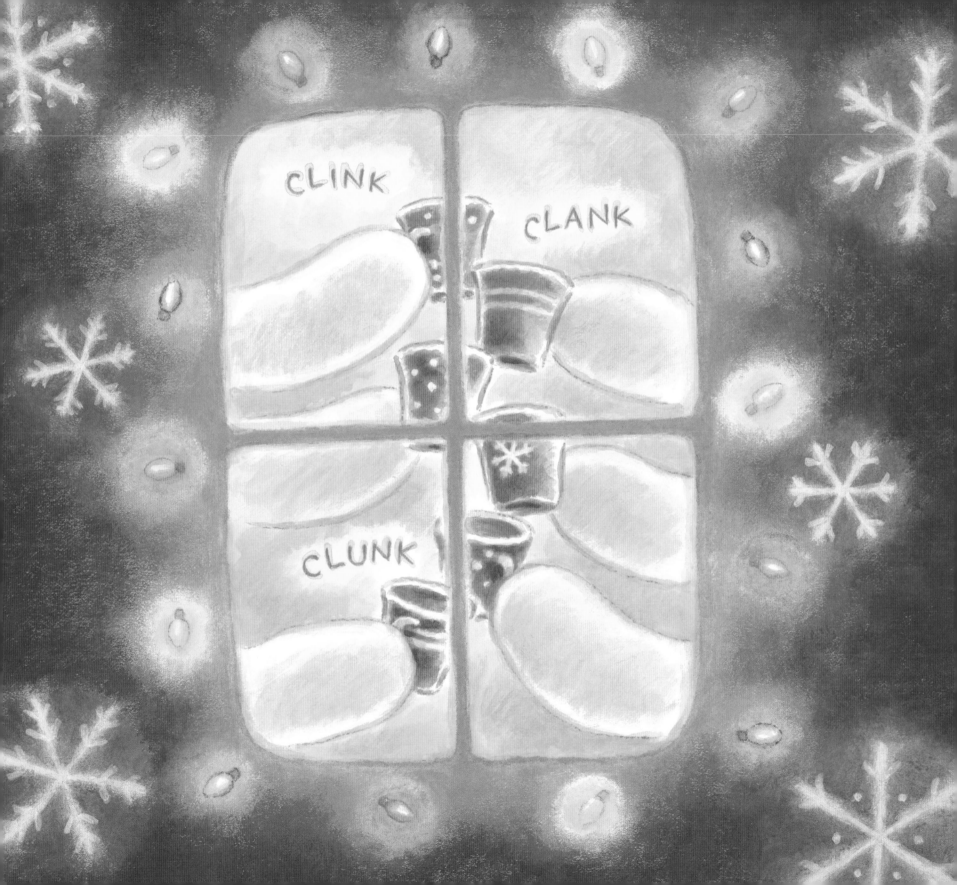